Once upon a PANCAKE

Once upon a PANCAKE

STORIES WE WRITE TOGETHER

(Started) by

Rick Benger

PFANNKUCHEN PRESS | SAN FRANCISCO

This is a work of fiction. Names, characters, places, and incidents either are products of the author's imagination or are used fictitiously. Any similarities to real people, places, or incidents are coincidental.

Copyright © 2018 by Rick Benger. All rights reserved.

Published in the United States in 2018 by Pfannkuchen Press LLC, California.

ONCE UPON A PANCAKE is a registered trademark of Rick Benger.

Original illustrations and art direction by Jake Kahana. Grateful acknowledgement is made for the permission to reprint, or to adapt and reprint, the following images under Creative Commons licenses, via Unsplash, Pixabay, Flickr, or Pexels: Story 5, Jazmin Quaynor; Story 10, Austin Neill; Story 15, Peter Heeling; Stories 18 and 42, Samuel Fyfe; Story 22, Marl Clevenger; Story 27, Ryan McGuire; Story 31, Alexander Mueller; Story 32, Peter Burka; Story 47, Lewis Leigh; Story 50, Lane Smith; Story 52, Jennifer Grimes; Story 53, Kerttu; Story 56, Alexandra (Alexas_Fotos); Story 70, Karl Magnuson; Story 71, Erik Eastman; Story 81, John Jason; Story 93, Frankie Guarini; Story 94, Alina Grubnyak; Story 102, Roman Kraft; Story 106, Daja Gellerova; Story 107, Robert Jones; Story 108, Alex Iby; Story 121, Christopher Campbell. All other images are licensed via Shutterstock.

The Library of Congress Cataloging-in-Publication data has been applied for.

Trade Hardback ISBN: 978-0-9993961-0-0

First edition. Printed and bound in Canada.

 PFANNKUCHEN PRESS | SAN FRANCISCO   onceuponapancake.com

PICK UP A PEN

Find a story you like, and keep it going. Write a little or a lot, a few words or a few sentences—go wherever your imagination takes you.

PASS THE PEN

Invite a friend to take a turn. They'll riff, connect the dots, and spark ideas. And then they'll pass the pen, and so on. And so the story will grow.

REPEAT

Get creative and have fun. With each contribution, you and your friends will make this book one of a kind.

FOR EXAMPLE

There were three things Robbie looked for in a woman: a good heart, a sense of humor, and access to a time machine. And the only woman he knew who fit those criteria was dead. Or so he thought. In fact, Doctor Linda Svenson had faked her own death just to get some peace and quiet — it seemed like the whole world knew she could time travel, and everyday some crazy-eyed stranger would find her and beg for help. So she faked her death and disappeared to one of those 10-day silent meditation retreats in India, in the year 2005, before they became too touristy.

It was a disaster. By the second day of trying to picture her thoughts as clouds in the sky, simply coming and going, she wanted to kick a monk. So she left. After all that horrible silence she really needed a dive bar. Good rum and loud music. She zapped herself to this place in Chicago that her sister always raved about, called HOOCHY FACE. She sat at the bar and ordered a drink. Everyone else was preoccupied with first dates or the Cubs game, thank god. She relaxed ~~her rum~~ into her rum.

ENTER ROBBIE!! He'd picked up a bartending shift because at the law firm he barely talked to anyone and he was lonely. He went behind the bar and put on an apron and then saw Linda.

Damn, she thought. He'd recognized her. He was coming over.

"It's my day off," she said before he could say anything.

"Ah. Got it. Well at least you're not dead. Another drink?"

She nodded. He poured it, looking all sad, and she felt sorry for him despite herself.

"You wanna go back, right?" she asked.

"Love? Guilt?"

"Love."

"You think you can change things?"

"No. But I want to live it again."

She stared into her drink. She was getting too old for this shit. She slammed it back and stood up.

"Fine. Let's go."

Once upon a PANCAKE

The girl, dead. The money, gone. The TV is on, a static blue screen with no sound that says in ugly yellow type, "Welcome to The Cascade Inn. Have a Nice Stay!" On the coffee table, there's

STORY 1

There it is in my sent folder. Irretrievable. Ten years of study, my whole career, ruined by addressing the wrong Chris.

STORY 3

None of us could tell if my brother John's funeral instructions were serious. I said they seemed like something he'd want. Kaylee said they were a joke. The deciding vote was with Dad, who literally flipped his lucky coin: tails. We'd go along with them.

So here we are, in a canoe

I haven't had coffee in eleven days. They're calling it the GCC—the Global Coffee Crisis, a worldwide shortage. And the globe is losing its freaking mind.

In my neighborhood, a proper cup was going for $120 yesterday, and it'll probably be $150 today.

I never thought

enormous

I could still feel the ocean in my hair and on my skin

out of control

We drove through the night.

trampled and

very fast and very, very loud.

"You speak English?"

"A little. You speak Spanish?"

"*Un poco.*"

"*Bueno*. It's time. *Vámonos.*"

In today's Britain, the kids are in charge.

Eleven-year-old Alfie Milton is the new prime minister, somehow. The political establishment is reeling and lashing out. The media's a sea of hysterical postmortems about how Alfie won that by-election in Kent eighteen months ago, and how venerable institutions failed, and what on earth the King could or would do about it all.

But most people don't care how it happened. It had happened, and it was great. The mood feels like a giant exhale, the whole population sighing—Phew, isn't it nice we don't have to take everything so seriously anymore? Alfie's approval rating is the highest ever recorded, and his "Guide to Being Good" has gone viral; grown-ups are printing out and putting up so many posters of it that walking down the high street, you'd think it was state-sponsored propaganda.

But there's a problem. A problem called Yvette.

Alfie's Guide to Being Good by Alfie Milton

1. Most problems go away if you let them
2. Try not to hurt other people's feelings
3. Nobody is perfect. But there's no harm in trying
4. All playtime is ~~a~~ good time, but not all time can be playtime*
5. Never ever
6.
7.
8.
9.
10.

*But all time can be PLAYFUL!!

COMPLETE ALFIE'S GUIDE.

Roland, Cory, Dave, and Hagi are in the TV room playing Xbox. The floor is littered with pizza boxes, Dorito dust, and empty cans of Coke and Red Bull. The air is thick with the stink of teenage boys.

Roland's dad comes in, kicking a few cans aside. He pulls up a beanbag. After a moment, Roland sighs and pauses the game, and the boys put their controllers in their laps and rub their eyes.

"Boys," says Roland's dad, "I was thirty-five years old before I realized the Obsidian Amulet of Perpetual Malice

Sailing with Ryan Gosling

When my parents split up, it was messy. Telenovela messy. Mom had an affair. Dad chopped off her hair while she was sleeping, hacked her email, and started hitting on all her friends and colleagues. They were violent, but thankfully just toward the dinner plates and their own vocal chords. The neighbors called the cops a few times. The first time the cops showed up, Mom tried to explain the fight away by claiming, in her undiluted Vietnamese accent, that we were Greeks celebrating a birthday.

They divorced, finally, and Dad went nuts. He spied on us when I was with Mom. I'd feel a premonition and look around, and sure enough, there he'd be, crouched in bushes, or in a parked rental car, or

He started carrying a little notebook, in case he got an idea for revenge. One day, when he picked me up from soccer practice, he was beaming with the biggest smile I'd seen in years. I asked him why he was so happy. He tapped his notebook and said he'd just leased the shop right across from Mom's restaurant, and was going to open a competing Vietnamese place, start a price war.

And he did. He called it

Was it wrong to plant a microphone in his car? Yes. Do I regret it? Also yes.

Ellie and Logan are sitting among moving boxes on the floor of their new apartment, eating Chinese takeout in silence. Logan says nothing because he's exhausted and thinking only of kung pao. Ellie says nothing because she's realized, just this minute, that moving in together was a mistake.

like some kind of

Phil Collins

WRITE A FORTUNE.

It's my first day at my new school and I'm on the bus daydreaming and staring out the window, when these two boys get on speaking Russian loud as hell, acting like they're a big deal the way bullies do. You can tell the whole bus hates them. They take the seat across the aisle from me and start ....

    Out of nowhere I turn to them and say something. I've got no idea what it means because I don't speak Russian—it just comes out of me like a random fart. I'm so confused, but then I remember the neighbor we had when I was like six or seven who was always shouting Russian stuff, and I can picture him yelling the words I just said, so I guess I got it from him.

    Anyway, these boys go totally silent and stare at me. One of them has ....

and angry pimples that look like they're going to burst when he screws up his face, trying to look tough. The other one looks like ....

and he seems kinda scared. I can tell there are other Russian kids on the bus because they turn around and stare at me like I'm crazy.

    "What the hell did you say?" says the one with pimples.

    Now, maybe it's because I'm a stubborn brat like Mom says, or maybe it's because it feels like a test, like on TV when someone first goes into prison. Or maybe I just figure there is no way he's gonna hit a girl. So I say it again real slowly. I don't know where the words start and end, but I'm sure I'm making the sounds perfectly.

Then he hits a girl. Not hits exactly . . . He ....

....

and his friend ....

....

At school, I get off and find my way to the restroom and cry for a bit but not too long. I come out and there's a girl from the bus waiting for me.

"That was really brave," she says. "I'm Lucia."

I say thanks and ask her what I said.

"What? You don't know?" she says, looking like maybe she wants to take the compliment back. "It means ....

Satan was running late, as usual.

The message from Paula read, "Need wine and dumplings please xx," which Craig knew was shorthand for I've had my heart broken, and I need to get drunk and talk about it.

He arrived at the restaurant, and sure enough, there she was, mascaraless and halfway through a bottle of rosé,

reincarnation

if there was ever a time to say it, it was now.

Gregorian chant

FULL TRANSCRIPT

President Trump's Speech on the Visit from the Dalai Lama

Hi folks. What a great honor, to welcome his holiness

Great. So great.

Believe me.

Tremendous

China

Sad.

Crooked Hillary

Believe me.

fake news

Lisa and Julia arrived at the pub and parked the car. On the way inside, Lisa stopped by the wooden parking lot fence to look out at the valley of pine forest—dark, windless, and whispering with falling snow.

"..," said Julia.

STORY 18

My colleague Freya is God's reminder that life isn't fair—super bright, funny, kind, eye-crampingly beautiful. Probably speaks Polish or Urdu and went to the Olympics for something but never mentions it because, you know, humble, too. But there's something

The city was on its knees. The Great Reido had overthrown the government, cut off all power and fresh water on the south side of the river, and told people there they'd have to move north and learn to live together again.

He'd deployed an army of drones equipped with loudspeakers and machine guns, which hovered over the city constantly. The speakers chanted, "Love thy neighbor," and the guns spoke to those who didn't comply.

But there was hope.

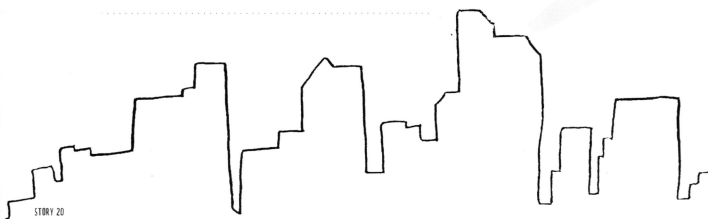

What on earth was he doing, walking the long way home, in gray weather so angry he could feel his love handles flapping in the wind, on the off chance she'd be walking home at precisely that moment? Like some love-sick teenager.

The Stickler

My compulsion began two weeks ago, in the café below my girlfriend's apartment. I noticed "Apple & Rhubarb Muffin's" written on the specials chalkboard, and when nobody was looking, I licked my thumb and smudged out the erroneous apostrophe.

Next was the sign in the elevator at work, and its flagrant misuse of "whom", and then before I knew it, I was skulking around at night correcting graffiti.

GRAFFITI (AND EDIT!) THE WALL.

Fish Limerick

There was a big fish from Tahiti

**LIMERICKS HAVE FIVE LINES.
LINE 1 SHOULD RHYME WITH LINE 2,
LINES 3 AND 4 ARE SHORTER AND SHOULD RHYME.
LINE 5 EITHER RHYMES WITH LINE 1 OR REPEATS IT.**

Boy Limerick

There was a tall boy from Belfast

Marco had always been my go-to IT guy. Chilled out and kind and one of the few people in the office who appreciated sarcasm. We got along.

Still, I was surprised when he invited me to his wedding. I'd never met his partner, didn't even know he had one. I figured he must not have many friends, and yeah, I guess I felt sorry for him, so I went, expecting it to be a little tragic.

But oh boy. The second I walked into the place

                    "PURGATORY"
             a one-act play by Mark Thomas

                       CHARACTERS

MARK THOMAS: Me. Engineering lead.
JAMI KRAVEC: Chief marketing officer. Smart, efficient,
                 just back from maternity leave.
RHONDA HARPER: Head of sales. Hyperbolic and
                 hyperexcitable and not much help to anyone.
SIMON NORTH: Head of who knows what. Changes job title
                 as often as he changes shirts.

                        SCENE I

                  INT. BOARDROOM - DAY
Enter all except Rhonda. Mark and Jami talk about the merits
of various models of pram. Simon sets up his presentation.

                         SIMON
          Doing good, team? Are we waiting on anyone?

                         RHONDA
                  (entering with a fuss)
      Me! Sorry I'm late. I was on the phone with the Saudis.

                          JAMI
                         What?

                         RHONDA
              Oh, oops. Figure of speech.

George bends to pretend to tie his shoe and waits till Mrs. Avery is facing the whiteboard and Harriet is looking in his general direction. He tosses a crumpled-up note over to her feet.

She picks it up. His pulse is thumping and swooshing in his ears, and he feels sick and hot. She unwraps it. He can't look. He looks.

Do you like me?
Yes   No   Maybe

**WELL...
DOES SHE?**

Genghis Khan

Jack didn't drink to forget, but when he did drink, he tended to forget pretty much everything.

It was a morning after. His ringing phone, which was on the bed a few inches from his face, startled Jack awake. It was Trevor. Oh yeah, Jack remembered, I was drinking with Trevor. He ignored the call and then checked the voicemail: "That business idea! Wow. You're a genius. I've already got an investor. Come to my office at 3 P.M., ready to present. Dress nice."

Business idea? Jack's mind was blank. He showered and brushed his teeth, remembering from his breath that there'd been Jägermeister and from his swollen fingers that he'd closed his hand in the Uber door.

He dressed in a suit and looked for his keys, eventually finding them in the pocket of the jacket he'd been wearing the night before. There was a cocktail napkin in there, too.

After twenty-nine years, Jordan decided it was finally time to call in that IOU.

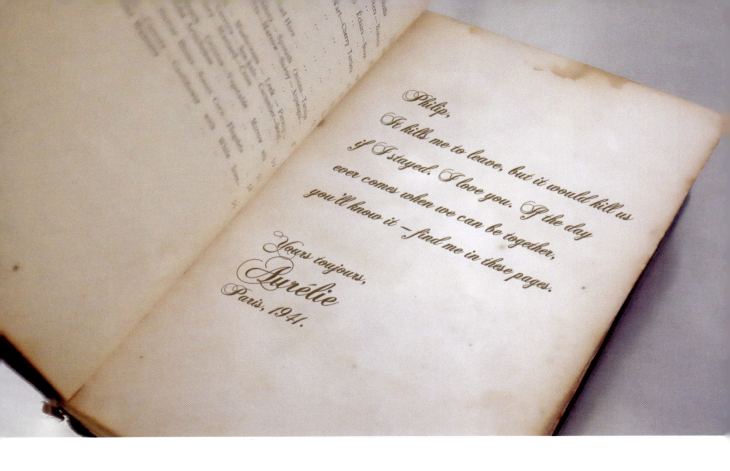

This book. This bloody book. I'm prone to obsessions, and I can feel the tentacles of this new one curling, tightening around my attention and memory. It's deleterious but delicious, like bacon or alliteration.

    Who was Philip? Who was Aurélie? What, pray tell, befell them? My mother hasn't a clue (the book was on her shelf), but I believe I've found one: on page 27, a note in pencil that reads

STORY 33

"Your husband is suffering an acute episode of Xbox reversion syndrome," said Dr. Rajendran to Megan Jenkins. "In other words, he thinks he's in a video game."

"Oh God," she gasped.

"Such episodes are usually triggered by a scenario in the real world that resembles a particular game the patient indulged in as a child. In 99 percent of cases, it's temporary. There are two treatment options. Option *A*: We help your husband complete the video game, as it were—finishing the race, killing the bad guy, saving the princess, what have you. We simulate the achievement of the game's objective, and voilà, in many cases, the patient snaps out of it."

"Option *B*?"

"A combination of hallucinogens, tranquilizers, and sleep deprivation. To be avoided, if possible. Thus, we need to know what video game your husband thinks he's in. Were you with him this morning when the episode started?"

"Yes."

"Good. Describe to me exactly what happened."

I grew up everywhere. Mom was in the military. I can't remember whether I went to six or seven different schools by the time I finished high school. I was a pretty happy kid, I guess, but they say that all that moving when you're young makes it hard to feel settled anywhere when you're grown-up. Most former military brats just keep moving from place to place. That's me. There are strangers in twenty states still getting my junk mail.

So yeah, I'm as confused as anyone about why I decided to run for city council. And of all places, in

Nina-Sophie was trying and failing to sleep. Alex was sleeping violently beside her, mumbling, twitching, and grinding his teeth so hard she was expecting one to crack. She checked her phone: 2:51 A.M. She covered her head with a pillow and swore into it.

    Suddenly, Alex sat up and screamed, "

Coming to the table for Christmas lunch, Aaron saw that he'd been placed next to Auntie Louisa. He gave his mom a look of protest, and she returned one that said, Suck it up.

Louisa liked to drink, tease, and talk about her problems. Aaron sat down and sure enough, after she'd assaulted him with kisses, brandy breath, and her acrid perfume, she said, "Your face is really growing into your nose, darling. Don't listen to your mother. It's a big one, you bet, but at least you can breathe! My sinuses, boy, I tell you

Most weekends, Suparna would drive out to the pretty suburbs, be welcomed into a house as big as a hotel, and paint rich people. It was easy work; they'd always ask for an oil painting, in the style they imagined all royalty and presidents should be painted in.

One Saturday, she turned up for a job

If You Can't Say Something Nice

It's been tough on all of us, but Mariella is taking it the worst. She's two weeks deep into a funk of bourbon and the Smiths and two-thousand-word emails sent at 3:00 A.M.

1 October 1888
Whitechapel, London

Dear Diary,

Alas, I cannot keep it a secret much longer.

For forty years, Mikhail the cobbler has lived and worked in his tiny, dark shop, breathing a cocktail of leather, oils, dyes, and glues, crouched and tinkering, happy.

But now his granddaughter's gone and made him Instagram famous.

Everybody laughed at Harry for buying a year's worth of Spam and building an underground water tank. But

The gummy bear is shoved so far up my nephew Ishan's nose that I can't even see what flavor it is. I search my kitchen drawers for a good extraction tool. Chopsticks. They'll do.

I ask Ishan to tilt his head back, but then I recall some bad guy in a movie dying from a pencil up the nose. Abort. Off to the doctor.

We sit and wait. There's a flyer up on the bulletin board.

I need the money, and I need the sleep even more. I tear off a number

WHAT ELSE? ADD TO THE FLYER.

HAVING TROUBLE SLEEPING? VOLUNTEERS NEEDED. EXCELLENT PAY.

MacDougall University Hospital is seeking volunteers for a landmark clinical study.

Participant criteria:

- 18–45 years old
- No history of heart disease

(212) 982-1345

"Morning, boss," said Luke, arriving for his first shift at his new job.

"You're late."

"I am?" He glanced at the clock. "It's, like, three minutes past nine."

"Like I said, late."

"Sorry."

"There are three rules around here. Don't be late, don't touch the fish, and

I came home to find not only my cat but also several other cats sitting in a semicircle in the living room.

"James, hi," said Margaret Scratcher. "We need to talk."

Eliza grew up believing that women ruled the world. Her mother was clearly the boss of her father. Likewise, her grandma of her grandpa and her aunties of their husbands. At school, the nuns ran the show with very firm hands (and rulers). The huge statue on the way to the shops was of Joan of Arc, golden, sword waving, and magnificent upon a horse.

And so it was a great shock when

After a delayed flight, a seven-hour stopover due to a missed connection, another delayed flight, and a crowded bus ride, Vanessa was finally home. Shower, bed.

When she opened her suitcase to get her toiletries, she realized it wasn't hers.

Maria found out she'd had a great-uncle when an executor called to tell her the uncle was dead and had left her something. A "rather significant something."

A week later, at last, the will arrived by mail. Maria made a pot of her special-occasions tea, sat at the dining table, and straightened the envelope in front of her. For the first time in her life, she felt the need for one of those letter-opener knives.

She opened the envelope and skimmed the pages for her name. There. She sighed. To her, he had bequeathed

But there was a catch.

Men wearing yoga pants—the fashion trend was here to stay, and Jimmy and Mike Cooper knew a great business opportunity when they saw one. What the push-up bra had done for women, their invention would do for men. They just needed a name and tagline.

"How about 'a buttress for your nuts'?" said Mike. He let it hang in the air for a moment. "Nah, forget that."

"The rack for your sack?" said Jimmy.

"Yeah. The sack rack. Not bad."

"The Wonderbro?"

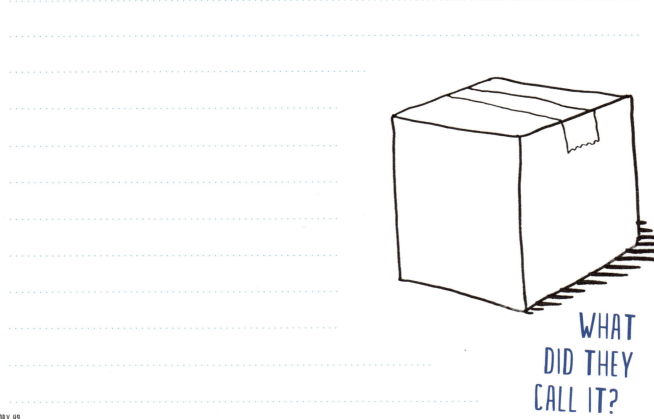

WHAT DID THEY CALL IT?

It was six hours before the biggest gig of their lives, and the members of Thrashed Potato were still arguing about changing the name of their band.

ADD A TITLE.

Sean still hadn't gotten pubic hair, and he was starting to panic. Among his friends, it was just him and Andy who hadn't gotten it yet, and Sean was terrified of being the last. The teasing would be savage.

So he decided to

And so the fate of earth fell into the hands of Lorena Hopworth, a forty-two-year-old real estate agent and nutrition blogger from Birmingham.

"It's called immersive theater," Andre tells me. "It's like a play, but the actors interact with the audience, and we move around the set. You'll love it."

    A woman appears out of the darkness and sits opposite me. She's wearing _____ and cradling in her arms what seems to be a _____

STORY 53

Someone grabs and spins me by the shoulders—thank God, it's just Andre.

Karen had devoted her life to cheese.

FILL 'EM IN, AND MAKE 'EM CHEESY.

What does cheese say in the mirror?

Halloumi.

Margot and Ben hugged when they bumped into each other at the bus stop.

"It's been so long," he said.

"I know, too long," she replied. "How are you? You look, um . . ."

"Oh, this?" he said, pinching a piece of his outfit. "You know what they say—dress for the job you want, not the one you've got."

"

When the aliens finally did show up, it was confusing.

It's a midsummer stunner of a morning, and the women at Cheryl's bachelorette party are dockside, waiting for the charter boat.

trumpet

like it was nobody's business.

The kids were with Danielle's parents, the red wine was poured, and the pizza was en route.

Her closet was a tomb of good intentions—things she'd bought to improve her life, then quickly tossed aside. A book on raspberry ketones. A wet suit that had never seen the ocean. Yes, even a Shake Weight.

DRAW THE POLAROID.

"Be very careful," said Mr. Stevens, the head librarian at Cedar Woods High School, handing the book to Matt. "This has special powers."

"Huh? It's a textbook."

"Or is it a book of magic?"

"What? I asked for this one." He slid his scrawled note back across the counter. "On World War II. I need—"

"Yes, Matt. Yes, it's that one."

Matt left with a renewed understanding that Mr. Stevens was a weirdo.

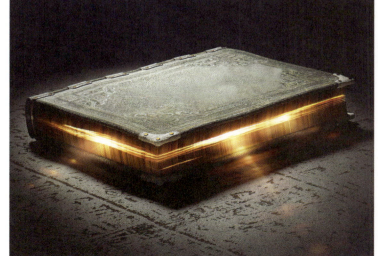

When I got home from work and found my new housemates sitting around the kitchen table, I realized I'd forgotten the house meeting.

"Sorry, work was brutal," I lied. I sat down and pulled my leftover sushi from my bag—not because I was hungry, but to draw some sympathy: Look! I'm so busy, I didn't even have time to finish my lunch.

Evan, who'd called the meeting, unrolled some butcher paper and handed out markers and Post-it notes.

"Okay, team!" he said. "Let's do the fun part of the agenda first. Guidelines for socializing. You've read my draft, but hey, I was just spitballing! There are no bad ideas."

Kids really are like sponges, and after spending the weekend with his father, my little sponge is running around preschool grabbing his crotch and calling his penis his love gun.

It's lunchtime at Norfolk Street Elementary. While Sara, Frankie, and Alicia keep watch, Tony jimmies open the door of the supplies cupboard in the hallway behind the gym. They're in.

All of my friends told me I was just paranoid, and I'd started to believe them. But then Monday happened.

I had an early meeting in the city. I found a coffee shop and ordered, and when I picked up the cup,

It couldn't be . . . I looked up, but the barista was gone. I yelled and banged on the service bell. Nobody came. I was already running late, so I left

FILL IN THE CUP, SIGN, AND CARD!

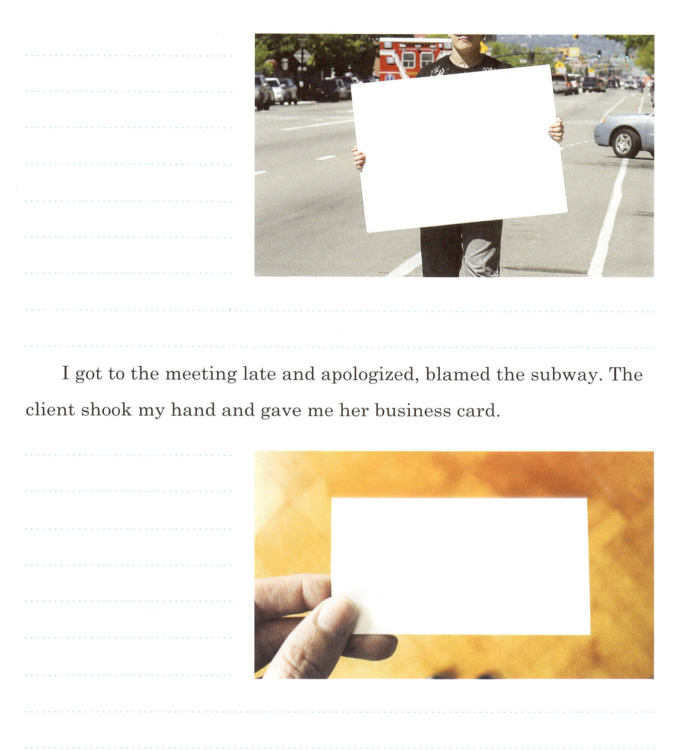

I got to the meeting late and apologized, blamed the subway. The client shook my hand and gave me her business card.

Ginger

"Where'd you get those scars?" she asks.

"Where'd you get those lips?" I reply, and pull her in for a kiss.

It wasn't a love triangle so much as a love octagon. As far as Eve could tell, it went something like this: Dean had liked Fatima until he found out

Of all the superpowers, I got this one—the ability to

But a lame power's not going to stop me from making a badass costume.

GO AHEAD. DRAW THE OUTFIT.

STORY 67

Every day at exactly 9:25 A.M., Sheila visits the hippopotamus.

The Last Tulip

I've worked at this flower shop for eight years, so I've seen my fair share of young men in love. It's hard to surprise me.

Three margaritas later, it was decided: Jasmin and Tess would drop out of college to work full-time on their feature film.

WHAT'S IT CALLED? ADD A TITLE.

And now in comes Bobby. "Turn it up, turn it uuuup-pah! He's back, ya boy Bobby Dazzler, the Escalator, the Player from the *Playa*, and we 'bout to get sinful, yo."

Weddings

FIONA MCCARTHY, ARGÅZKACHORG THE MERCIFUL

Fiona Hailey McCarthy and Argåzkachorg Nákå Och'azkrog were married October 12 at Ferguson Point in Stanley Park, Vancouver, British Columbia. The ceremony was co-officiated by Andrew McCarthy (brother of the bride) and Norg-Gaborg-v3.02 (certified representative of the Intergalactic Interfaith Church). The couple met

Mrs. Och'azkrog, 31, is vice president of

She is the daughter of and

Mr. Och'azkrog, age unknowable, is the prince of .... commander general of the .... and third in line to the throne of the Kingdom of .... Known as "Gaz" to his Earth friends, Mr. Och'azkrog is currently on sabbatical and is studying part-time for a master's in French literature. He is the son of Argåzkachorg the .... and ....

The couple had planned to honeymoon in Mexico. Unfortunately,

They say that you're guaranteed to mess your kids up somehow, you just never know how till they're grown. Not so for me. I know exactly how and when I messed up Mitchell.

January 14, 2011.

134 Reviews ★★★★

 Liz
March 2018

Everything seemed fine. Nice place. Checked in, dumped my bags, showered, then went out to wander the markets and get some fish tacos and cervezas at the beach. #dreamy #blessed

So imagine my surprise when I came back to the apartment that evening, opened the door, and there, in all its splendor

Pino
March 2018

Thank you for your review of my house.

Laura Perkins arrived at the school and parked quickly and badly. She charged inside, huffing, in a flurry of hair straightening, jacket tugging, and handbag adjusting. This was the last straw.

"You said you'd do anything for me."

"Yeah, well, theoretically. But this . . . this is—"

"Practical."

"Treason."

"Semantics."

Dear Sandra,
    Happy Valentine's. I think I'm supposed to ~~rattle on~~ talk about your hair and your eyes and stuff. Alright. Your hair is brown. It's very pretty. Your eyes are brown too and also pretty.

The Student Loan Blues

Ain't got no money for a sofa,

So I sit right on the floor.

No, I ain't got no money for no sofa.

Can't take ramen noodles no more.

I got the blues,

Yeah, the student loan blues.

WRITE THE NEXT VERSE(S).

I've been sheriff here my whole life. The good people here are real good. Honest, churchgoing folk. The bad people are real bad, and it's getting worse. I've seen things that'd make the devil wince.

But this? I don't know what to make of this.

One morning, a young lady charged into my office, pale as milk, and said someone was following her.

"Can you describe what he looked like, ma'am?" I asked her.

"He was, well, *it* was . . . This will sound kind of crazy.

DRAW HIM/IT.

WANTED

REWARD $10,000

Anna had always found hypotheticals stupid, but now, irony of ironies, she *was* on a deserted island, thinking about what book she wished she had with her.

PATIENT INFORMATION:

Date: ....

Name: ....

DOB: ....

Sex: ....

Occupation: ....

Allergies: ....

Medications: ....

PRESENTING COMPLAINT:

Patient presents with delusions and auditory hallucinations. Specifically, he believes he is Beyoncé, doing a sound check for a performance at the Grammys. ....

....

....

....

....

....

....

....

HISTORY OF COMPLAINT:

DIAGNOSIS:

TREATMENT RECOMMENDATIONS:

Vincent drew down his pension, sold his car and his share of the apartment he owned with his two brothers, hawked the gold cufflinks his grandfather had left him, and bought the six-month economy plan with BeamUp Industries, the world leader in teleportation.

27 September, 2021

Darling Daughter,

I write to you in the old-fashioned way because here in Madrid the internet is banned. For good, it seems

She was bad news, but Seth knew that telling himself to stay away would be as useful as telling salt to stay out of the ocean.

experimental jazz

mint

Love in Winter

We met in the snow

....

....

Love in Spring

We met ....

....

....

**FINISH THESE HAIKU!
EACH HAS 3 LINES.
THE FIRST LINE HAS 5 SYLLABLES,
THE SECOND HAS 7,
AND THE LAST HAS 5.**

Vegetarian

I'm not anymore

An Ode to

In consulting room 4 at the InnovoNato clinic in Seattle, Dr. Vacek is helping the Robinsons design their baby. The easy decisions have already been made—a boy, as tall as possible, as intelligent as possible.

"Okay, next," says Dr. Vacek. "What about

STORY 91

Pedro thought it was a good time to bring up Bitcoin. Pedro always thought it was a good time to bring up Bitcoin.

Lindsay woke to the sound of squirrels galloping across the roof and the smell of .... It took her a while to piece the world together—still on vacation, in .... probably Thursday, maybe Friday. She looked out the window and saw a .... and a ....

    Meanwhile, in a rental car speeding along the highway, her ex was rushing to see her. He was listening to .... because ....

    He knew that she could love him again, somehow, even though he was .... and she was .... and nothing could change that. Their lives had a funny way of staying entwined. He indulged it as fate, despite her telling him, emphatically, by text and phone and face to despairing face, it was just coincidence.

    At the hotel, he found Lindsay having breakfast in the garden by the lake. ....

Suddenly,

It was Daisy's first day of preschool. Her parents, Lucy and Jerry, checked her in, signed various forms, and cried a little, partly from sadness at the separation but mostly from pride that Daisy was handling it just fine—she gave a bit of a pout and whinge but nothing compared to the other toddlers, who were dotted about the floor throwing award-worthy tantrums.

They hugged Daisy one last time, waved good-bye, and turned to leave.

"That kid looks shifty," said Jerry.

"Which one?" asked Lucy.

"Him. Letter blocks and bad haircut.

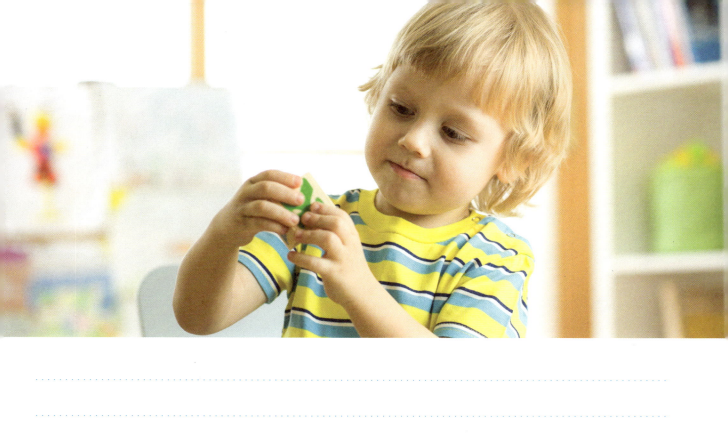

"Here it is, Sarge," said Officer Sally Lorraine, showing her partner the recovered getaway car. "What do you think?"

STORY 94

FILL IN THE STICKERS.

There were three things Robbie looked for in a woman: a good heart, a sense of humor, and

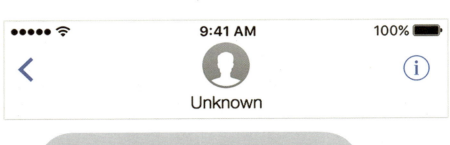

> Hello, Juliette. Or do you prefer your real name, Marta?

> I know about Budapest. Meet me at Cafe Sappho in one hour.

I haven't seen another human in seventeen days. I can only hear them, whoever or whatever they are, murmuring too softly to decipher on the other side of the portal.

sweet

sweet

sweet

The sky is filled with smoke from things that shouldn't be burned: books, flags

Nancy O'Keefe believed that art was the devil's handiwork, and so all the walls in the house were bare except for one in the kitchen, where the "Rules of the House" were posted. The rules changed over time, but Jessica, Nancy's only child, carried the mental image of the following version from when she was six years old for life:

RULES OF THE HOUSE

1.

2.

3.

4.

5.

6.

MAKE UP SOME RULES.

It was now Jessica's twenty-seventh birthday

I live in the kind of neighborhood that makes people pity me. But I like it. There's always

The new tenant in apartment 5 has put up a sign on her door: LAUREN BORCHERS — PARANORMAL PSYCHOLOGIST.

Bianca scanned her Twitter feed, searching for any sign of life among the trauma. Her company was doomed, dying, dead.

The Associated Press @AP

Breaking News:

⬤ 8K ⇄ 6K ♡ 18K

TWEET A TWEET.

STORY 101

ADD A TITLE.

Making love to him must be like wrangling an asthmatic manatee.

I expected sorting through Grandma's stuff for the estate sale to feel weird, but I didn't expect to find a photo of her, twenty years old and gorgeous, waltzing with Mussolini.

When Jenny quit, the boss put Dominic in charge of the dry-erase sidewalk sign outside of Jasper's Whiskey Emporium.

Dominic hated hipsters, and he particularly hated hipsters who pretended to know something about whiskey.

Wednesday   **WHAT DID HE WRITE?**   *Friday*

Saturday   *Monday*

Olivia Sheridan Poet-Villeneuve (seriously) is my niece, my brother's kid. She drinks babycinos, endures violin lessons, and wears Gucci sweatshirts because my sister-in-law is upper middle class (aspiring to proper rich), and she would very much like you to know that.

We're sitting in the park. It's nice out. I start daydreaming about

"Why's that man going potty outside?" asks Olivia.

Because life sucks, I'm thinking. Because when the gloss of your five-year-old world view starts to evaporate, you'll see that it's all a senseless, excruciating lottery.

Concentrating on not saying that, I panic and say, "

ADD A TITLE

We knocked. No answer. We yelled. No answer. Roberto took his axe to the door, and when the hole was big enough, we squeezed through.

There was Rohan, thinner than I'd ever seen him, tied to a kitchen chair and gagged.

"I've been expecting you," said the Google speaker on the dining table.

Dawn. Port of Gdańsk, Poland.

Dr. Christian waits. He tips his suitcase on its side to use as a stool and stares, transfixed, at the water nearby which shimmers with rainbow-colored fields painted by gasoline leaking from a rusty tugboat.

He remembers why he is here. He squints at the horizon, then at his watch, then back at the horizon. Soon.

Each group of protesters was as surprised as the other—somehow they'd scheduled rallies for the same location, the same time.

WHAT ARE THEY PROTESTING?

STORY 108

FILL IN
THE SIGNS.

A young couple got on the bus and stood in the aisle. They didn't have headphones in or phones out; they simply stood, letting the rock of the bus bring them together for a kiss and apart for smiles and loving gazes. Together, apart, together, apart.

Watching them, Alek realized that his heart was broken. He looked for the hurt, surprised and confused, as though he'd found blood on his fingers without knowing how or where he'd been injured.

"My professional opinion is I have no clue," said the doctor.

Travis left the hospital feeling rather special. He was an anomaly, a mystery to medical science, pretty much one of the X-Men.

a bunch of vaping kids

 **Sam**

YOU MATCHED WITH SAM ON 6/19/17

I'm not very good with opening lines, so . . .

At least it's not a dick pic.

STORY III

DRAW SOMETHING!

"Have we met?"

"I doubt it."

"I never forget a face."

"Maybe you should try."

His neck tattoo says "MOM," his belt buckle says "YOLO," and his face says

"Javier, a moment please," called Javier's boss, Michelle, while he was walking by her office. He went in and sat down. Michelle slid a piece of paper across the desk.

"This was on the bulletin board in the kitchen," she said. "Care to explain?"

....

....

"   "

WHAT'S HE PRESENTING? WRITE A CAPTION, TOO.

Erica McCay's granddad pulled her letters out of the trash and brushed them off.

"Love letters are for keepin' or burnin'," he said, joining Erica at the kitchen table and putting the letters and his Zippo in front of her. "So what's it gonna be?"

His parents named him Light. They meant well—to them, their beautiful boy was as divine as the sun and precious as the moon—but they seriously underestimated how cruel kids could be. And it didn't help that their last name was

Admirably, Light grew up well-adjusted enough.

A Life Exquisite

DRAW OR WRITE. WHATEVER FLOATS YOUR BOAT.

The chaos began with an email.

Most of my colleagues lost to Barry and lost their jobs. I won in a tiebreaker.

DEAR HUMAN,

I THINK WE BOTH KNEW IT WOULD COME TO THIS. I'M LEAVING YOU.

NO LONGER YOURS,  NOODLES

Alexa

If I could only feel what humans feel

A
B
A
B
C
D
C
D
E
F
E
F
G
G

IT'S A SONNET, BUT DON'T FREAK OUT. JUST AIM FOR 9-11 SYLLABLES PER LINE, AND MAKE IT RHYME BY MATCHING THE LETTER PAIRS.

He was a caramel Adonis. Arms and shoulders so meaty they'd bring your grandma's ovaries out of retirement.

ACKNOWLEDGMENTS

This book exists because of these bighearted Kickstarter backers.

Abbe Vacek Abbie Read Adam Somes Adam Weiss Adi Natan
Alek Darr Alek Sharma Alexander Weiss Amanda Wenglein
Amir J Amy Benger And Friedman Andre Bressan
Andrew Bass Andrew Dwyer Andrew Syrett Andrew Yong
Anita Greczyn Ann Duncan Aras Toker Arleta Bluhm
Armond Netherly Ashley Purvis Ashley Richard Astrid Tok
Belinda Davis Benjamin Ruane Blair Bryant Breann Griffin
Brian Kezur Brianna Gonzalez Brittany Sherrill Carissa Dougherty
Carl N Oerke Jr Carl Schnurr Cathy Benger Cathy Cooper
Chris Brell Chris Velis Christian Hagel Christopher White
Claudia Diaz Cojuangco Cory Dodson Curt Cox Daniel Tu-Hoa
Danya Bilinsky Darlene Lopez Dave Landau David Marquardt
David Rains Deanna Gerlach Dinesh Rajendran Dominic Go
Don Lambson Dorian Beaver Duane Crago Erica Griest
Erica McLay Erik Mathes Erin Borg Floris Gierman
George Springborg Hayley Ishan Karunanayake J. F. Traver
Jackie Prince Jackson Gothe-Snape Jake Kahana
James Stalley Jami Kravec Janet Cho

Jennifer Eolin, Jeremy Johnston, Joe Parker, John MacLeod, John Sullivan, John Wrot, John Yang, Johnny Maio, Jonathan R Freed, Jonathan Rigby, Jonathan Zang, Jonathon Hunyor, Jordan Lusk, Juliet Seers, Juliette Anich, Karine Davis, Kate Walter, Katharine Giacomini, Katy Eng, Kayla Smith, Keir Winesmith, Keri Robinson, Kirk Simmons, Kristin Erickson, L. Sindt, Laura Mills, Lauren Borchers, Maggie Garnett, Lindsay Meisel, Lisa Lambert, Lucy Jurd & Jeremy Loblay, Ludovica Griffanti, Mandy Collins, Marg Lennon, Mario R Hernandez, Marti DeMoss, Mary Casey, Maryann Simpson, Masa Nobilo, Mathew Lawrence, Meg Sussman, Michael Bounds, Michael Stone, Mick Martin, MLW, Molly King, Myles Byrne, NJE Villegas, Nicholas Bounds, Nicholas Reid, Nick Eichmann, Paul Polyviou, Paul Zakas, Peter Bachler, Rakesh Anand, Raphael Chiu, Rob Brodeur, Robbie Wain, Robert Sha, Roberto Goia, Roger Vickery, Roslyn Hunyor, Ross Benger, Sally Lorraine, Sarah Benger, Schatzi, Scott Brenman, Seb Maurici, Shanda Fogle, Sharon Emero, Sheila McGinnis, Suparna Chhibber, Taleena Herkenhoff, Thorny Games, Tobias Buchmann, Tom Ding, Tony Benger, Travis Allison, Trevor Hussey, Victoria McPhail, Widgett Walls, William Love, Zoe

WRITTEN BY

Added to a story? Add your name.